WHISPERS IN THE FOG

ARDEN SMITH

COPYRIGHT

Whispers in the Fog

AUTHOR'S NOTE

DISCLAIMER

The content of this novel, including themes of mystery, paranormal, and romance, is intended for entertainment purposes only. The author does not endorse any beliefs, practices, or ideologies associated with the supernatural or paranormal, as depicted in this fictional work.

The reader is advised that the scenes involving supernatural and suspense elements are purely fictional and are not intended to promote or suggest any real-life actions or beliefs.

Characters and scenarios depicted are not based on real events or people, and any similarity to actual persons, living or dead, or to actual events is purely coincidental.

TABLE OF CONTENTS

Copyright 2

Author's Note 3

Disclaimer 5

Chapter 1: Return to Eldermere 8

Chapter 2: The Historian's Warning 26

Chapter 3: Unveiling the Curse 42

Chapter 4: Secrets in the Fog 50

Chapter 5: Unmasking the Facade 60

Chapter 6: Confrontation at the Lighthouse 68

Epilogue 82

CHAPTER 1

RETURN TO ELDERMERE

The bus doors hiss shut behind Clara. Through the thick fog, the vehicle's taillights blur into red smears, then vanish.

Clara clutches her press badge in her pocket - a habit from five years of investigative reporting in Boston. The credential had opened countless doors, but here in Eldermere, she suspects it might not have the same level of success.

The terminal's flickering light casts strange shadows across empty benches worn smooth by generations of travelers. Salt-laden wind carries the mournful cry of distant foghorns, and beneath that, something else - a sound almost like whistles... or whispers.

Uncertain why she feels so uncomfortable, Clara's hand tightens on her bag strap. She pulls out her phone, checking the email from the lawyer one more time. "Your grandfather's property in Eldermere..."

The words still don't make sense. In thirty years, her mother had never once mentioned a grandfather, let alone one who owned property in this coastal town that seemed to exist in its own pocket of perpetual twilight.

"Excuse me?" Her voice catches as a woman hurries past. The woman keeps her face low. She pulls her coat tighter and quickens her pace.

A man reading a newspaper on the bench turns away when Cara approaches. He pretends he doesn't see her.

Feeling a rising frustration, Clara turns to another pedestrian, who crosses to the opposite side of the street. Clara's pulse quickens with each rejection.

A few days after she received the will saying her grandfather had left her a journal and his cottage, Clara had decided, on a whim to visit the little seaside town.

She'd done some research about the town. The visitor's guide she'd found online had painted Eldermere as a quaint fishing village with "rich maritime history and authentic coastal charm."

But the reality before her feels different - buildings hunched against the coast like guilty secrets, windows with dark, unwelcoming eyes.

Weather-beaten signs creak on rusted chains, their fade-worn letters spelling out business names that seem frozen in time: *"Fletcher's Maritime Supplies"* and *"The Rusty Anchor Pub"* - establishments that look like they haven't changed since the town's founding.

Even the air feels different here - heavier, as if the fog is releasing more than just moisture. It coats her throat with each breath, filling her mouth with the taste of salt, seaweed, and something metallic she can't quite identify.

The terminal light buzzes, dims, then brightens again. Her fingers fumble with her phone, muscle memory trying to pull up GPS. The signal bars dance between one and zero.

The map loads in chunks, digital pixels struggling against whatever force seems to dampen all modern conveniences here.

The Seaside B&B appears and disappears as the screen stutters, its location taunting her from three blocks east. Or is it West? In this fog, every direction feels like a betrayal of basic geography.

Just great! She's covered wars, exposed corruption, and faced down corporate thugs - but something about this town's silence fills her with a primal unease she can't rationalize away.

Her journalistic instincts, honed through years of investigating stories others wanted buried, scream that Eldermere itself is the biggest story she's ever encountered.

The cobblestones glisten black with moisture, seeming to absorb what little light remains.

Somewhere in the fog, a door creaks. Footsteps echo on stone, then stop. Clara spins around, her breath coming in short bursts. No one there.

"Hello?" The words stick in her throat. "Please. Can anyone tell me where to find the Seaside B&B?"

The footsteps start again, closer this time. A shadow moves at the edge of her vision. Clara involuntary steps back toward the terminal light until her shoulders hit the cold metal pole.

The shadow detaches itself from the darkness. "Wha' brings ye 'ere then?" The voice cuts through the silence, rough as barnacles, with an accent that seems to belong to a different century.

"I-I'm looking for the Seaside B&B." The words tumble out, her voice barely a whisper. She forces herself to maintain eye contact, even as her instincts scream to look away from those too-bright eyes.

His eyes glint like wet shells in the dim light. "Follow."

He turns, melting into the mist. Clara's feet move without her permission, drawn into his wake. The fog seems to thicken with each step, pressing against her face, cold and damp as a corpse's touch.

Every few seconds, the man looks back as if to confirm she is still following.

Each glance he sends her way lasts longer than the last. Every time his eyes run over her, she feels like a piece of meat at a butcher's market.

Her throat constricts. Clara glances back, subconsciously measuring how far they've walked from the terminal. She can't see more than a few inches in this thick fog, but it might be safer to take her chances of escape.

Just as she's about to make a dash back toward the terminal, the man stops.

One arm rises from his side, pointing upward into the darkness. Clara follows his gesture. The fog parts like a curtain, revealing a weather-beaten sign swinging on rusted chains: "Seaside Bed & Breakfast."

"Best do what ye came and leave." His breath mingles with the mist. "If ye know what's good for yar."

Between one heartbeat and the next, the fog swallows him whole, leaving Clara alone with the creaking sign and an ever-rising tide of her fear.

The brass doorknob turns smoothly under Clara's trembling fingers, warm to the touch despite the evening chill. Light spills onto the stoop in a golden rectangle, bringing with it the scent of cinnamon and butter - scents that seem impossibly normal after the otherworldly fog outside.

"There you are!" Mrs. Thompson, all bosom and swaying hips, comes toward her with the warmth of fresh-baked bread and concern.

She's a study in contradictions - her floral apron and flour-dusted hands speak of comfort and home, while her eyes hold the same shadowed knowledge Clara's seen in every face since stepping off the bus. When she smiles, it doesn't quite reach those eyes.

Gratefully, Clara pushes the door shut behind her and steps inside.

The sitting room beyond feels like a step back in time— oil paintings of ships battling angry seas, delicate porcelain figurines of lighthouse keepers' wives awaiting their husbands' return, and the subtle scent of salt and age everywhere beneath the more immediate aroma of baking.

"I've been watching for you since the bus was due." Her hands flutter around Clara like butterflies, unwinding her scarf, helping with her coat. "Goodness, you're chilled to the bone."

The fire crackles in the sitting room hearth, casting dancing shadows that feel nothing like the ones outside. Mrs. Thompson steers Clara into a plush armchair, its worn velvet embracing her in its comfort.

"Now then." Mrs. Thompson's slippers whisper against the hardwood floor as she hurries back and forth. A delicate China cup appears, steam rising from rich hot cocoa. A plate follows, bearing a slice of apple pie still warm from the oven. "Nothing sets the world right like soul food."

Clara wraps her fingers around the cup, feeling sensation return to her numb hands. Mrs. Thompson chatters about the weather, about Clara's journey, about the fresh cream she whipped for the pie. Her voice fills the cozy room like music, and the tension in Clara's shoulders begins to seep out.

The grandfather clock in the corner marks each peaceful moment with gentle ticks. Clara watches the fog press against the window panes, now seeming more like a soft blanket than grasping fingers.

Perhaps she had imagined the hostility at the terminal, the strange man's threatening manner. Perhaps—

The floorboards above her head creak, and Mrs. Thompson's stream of cheerful words stops mid-sentence.

Just for a moment, just long enough for Clara to notice, before the older woman launches into a story about her prize-winning apple trees.

"Your room's just up these stairs." Mrs. Thompson's voice echoes off the Victorian wallpaper, its faded roses climbing toward ornate crown molding. The staircase creaks beneath their feet, each step worn smooth by generations of footfalls.

The brass number seven gleams on a navy blue door. Inside, lace curtains frame a window seat overlooking the harbor. A brass bed dominates the space, its quilt a patchwork of seafaring motifs—ships, lighthouses, and compass roses.

An antique writing desk sits in the corner, water stains marking its surface like tide pools.

Once alone, Clara unpacks the few items of clothing she brought along before she settles into the window seat, her grandfather's journal heavy in her lap.

The leather is cracked in a pattern that speaks of frequent handling, the pages wavy from sea air, and what looks like water damage—though some stains are darker and rustier than mere water would leave.

Her fingers trace his initials embossed on the cover: *T.B. Thomas Bennett.* A man she should have known, should have grown up visiting on holidays and summers. Instead, he's a total stranger who chose to leave her his journal.

The first few entries are mundane - weather reports, tide tables, and notes about town council meetings. But around page thirty, the tone shifts:

"June 15th: Third time this week the harbor masters refused to discuss the Meridian incident. Says the records were lost in the '82 flood. But I've seen them in his office, locked in that brass-bound chest he thinks no one knows about. What's worth hiding after all these years?

June 18th: Mary Cooper crossed the street when she saw me coming. Second person this week. They know I'm asking questions. The fog's been thicker lately. Sarah at the diner says it's just weather patterns, but the way she said it... like she was reciting from a script.

June 20th: Found the old lighthouse logs. Pages are missing - specific dates. Every seven years, like clockwork. Same dates, the fog rolls in thickest. Same dates people tend to go missing."

The fog outside presses closer as if trying to read along. Clara pulls the curtains shut before she feels comfortable enough to settle down and continue reading the journal.

Her journalist's eye catches details others might miss. Dates that don't align. Names scratched out with such force the pen tore the paper. Locations mentioned repeatedly: the lighthouse, the caves, the old fishing dock. Her grandfather's normally precise handwriting grows erratic in later entries, as if written in haste – or fear.

Her eyes follow her fingers on the browned paper.

October 15th: They're watching me. I know too much. But I can't stop now. The pattern is clear – every seven years, like clockwork. But why? And how many others knew and stayed silent?

October 17th: The ledger proves everything. God help me, what have I uncovered? What have I been part of?

The words blur as Clara's eyes grow heavy. Images formed by words from the journal seep into her dreams. The dream shifts and twists like the fog itself.

Clara sees her grandfather, but younger than in any photo she's seen. He stands at the lighthouse door, scribbling frantically in his journal. The pages bleed ink like black tears.

"The pattern," he mutters, "always the pattern. Seven years. Seven souls. Seven secrets."

He looks up, sees her, and his face contorts in terror. "Clara! You have to understand - it's not just disappearances. The town... the fog... they're connected. It's all connected!"

Dark figures emerge from the mist behind him, their shapes almost human but wrong - too fluid, too tall. Their fingers stretch like smoke.

"Your mother was right to leave," he calls out. "But wrong to stay silent. The truth... in the lighthouse... the ledger proves..."

The shadows overtake him, and Clara tries to scream but the fog pours into her mouth, tasting of salt and copper and centuries of secrets.

The dream shifts.

Her grandfather runs toward her through the swirling mist. His face is twisted in terror, his coat flapping behind him like broken wings.

"Clara! Run!"

She tries to move, but her feet won't respond. Dark figures emerge from the fog behind him, their faces hidden in shadow.

"You have to run!" He's almost reached her. His hand stretches out—

The shadows overtake him. He crumples, his eyes finding hers one last time. "Run..." The word bubbles from his lips as he slumps forward—

Clara jerks awake, sitting bolt right on the bed. Weak morning light filters through the lace curtains. The journal lies open on her lap, her grandfather's last entry a stark warning: *Some secrets are kept in blood.*

Frightened, Clara shoved the journal far from her.

***

Hot water cascades over Clara's shoulders, but it can't wash away the lingering unease from her dream. Steam mists the bathroom mirror, reminding her of the fog outside.

Three months since the lawyer handed her the will and journal, his face pinched as he'd explained her inheritance – a cottage in a town she hadn't known was on the map, left by a grandfather who she'd never heard of.

Something about this town feels wrong. Like there's something more than buildings and streets hiding in the fog.

Morning light filters through the lace curtains, but the fog remains - always the fog. Clara's hands shake slightly as she buttons her blouse, her dream still clinging like cobwebs to her mind.

Outside her door, smells of fresh coffee and fresh blueberries pull her toward the dining room.

Mrs. Thompson hums as she sets out delicate china cups painted with lighthouse scenes

"Good morning, Mrs. Thompson."

"Oh just call me Mildred. Sleep well, dear?" Mrs. Thompson pours coffee into a delicate cup and sets a steaming stack of pancakes on the table.

Clara moves a pile into a small dish and pours a generous share of syrup. She cuts into the pancakes, savoring their buttery sweetness. She takes a healthy gulp from the mug to push it down.

"The fog can be... unsettling... for visitors. Such strange dreams it brings sometimes."

Clara's head snaps up. "Dreams?"

"Oh, just old wives' tales." Mrs. Thompson busies herself with the coffee pot, but Clara notices how her hands tremble. "They say the fog carries memories. Silly, of course. More coffee?"

The grandfather clock in the corner ticks with solemn precision. Clara counts seven chimes before asking, "Mrs. Thompson, how long have you run this place?"

"Oh, ages." The older woman's laugh sounds forced. "Since George and I... since George..." She stops, that same vacant look crossing her face that Clara's seen when anyone discusses the town's history.

The shuffling footsteps overhead make them both freeze. Something thunks against the floor upstairs - seven times, like counting. Mrs. Thompson's face goes pale.

Clara swallows, instantly knowing she will not be able to take another bite of food. "I was hoping to visit my grandfather's cottage today."

"Oh, you can't miss it." Mrs. Thompson brightens. "Just follow Harbor Street past the old cannery. It's the one with the blue—"

The front door groans open.

A man shuffles in, his movements are jerky and unnatural. His skin has a grayish tinge, dark circles ringing vacant eyes. Clara's fork clatters against her plate as she pushes back from the table.

Mrs. Thompson goes rigid, her coffee pot frozen mid-pour. The man drags past their table without acknowledgement, his breathing raspy and wet.

After he leaves the room, she flashes Clara an overly bright smile. "Oh, never mind him." Mrs. Thompson's voice quivers. "That's just... just Mark Thompson. My husband. Have more coffee."

But her hands are trembling so much that coffee spills over the cup's rim, spreading across the white tablecloth like a dark, ominous stain.

Clara lunges for a napkin, dabbing at the spreading coffee stain. Mrs. Thompson's hands are still trembling as Clara guides her into a chair. Neither mentions the shuffling footsteps that echo from above.

***

It's midmorning by the time Clara wraps a bright blue flannel around her neck and pulls on a matching wool cap.

As she steps out of Mrs. Thompson's cottage, the sun seems to be forcing its light into the day. The fog steps back slightly, though it still clings to the corners of buildings like cobwebs.

She follows Harbor Street past weathered storefronts – Eldermere Maritime Museum, Fletcher's Fishing Supplies, The Rusty Anchor Pub.

Each window display tells a story: salvaged ship parts, yellowed photographs of long-ago wrecks, newspaper clippings found treasure.

Then, without warning, the back of her neck prickles. Clara has been a journalist long enough to know when she is being followed.

She quickens her pace, her footsteps echoing off the weathered storefronts. Something shifts in her peripheral vision. She glances at a shop window's reflection – a shadow moves behind her, ducking behind a stack of lobster traps.

Heart pounding against her ribs, she forces herself to keep walking, fighting the urge to run or look over her shoulder. More movement, closer now. The scrape of shoes on wet stone.

She needs just the right moment to take this person by surprise. She wasn't even certain why they were following her.

Clara pretends to study a display of nautical equipment, watching the glass for movement. There, a figure stands half-hidden between buildings. He has unkempt sandy hair and thick glasses. His gaze meets hers in the reflection, unnaturally intense.

She spins around. "Hey!"

Footsteps scatter like startled birds. By the time she reaches the alley, only a puddle ripples, disturbed by recent movement.

"You! Stop!" But the fog swallows her voice.

Clara backs away, her shoulders tight. Every doorway could hide the watcher. Or someone working with them. She hurries forward, no longer trying to hide her fear.

A door slams somewhere behind her, causing Clara to hasten her steps. She reaches the cannery, its rusted walls looming over her. A plaque catches her eye – the *SS Meridian* lost with all hands in 1887. Below it, scratched words send a chill down her spine: *They never found the bodies.*

Though referring to the ship and its crew, they echo ominous in her ears.

Walking so fast she almost breaks into a run, Clara doesn't look back until she spots her grandfather's cottage exactly where Mrs. Thompson had described it would be.

The cottage sits on a bluff overlooking the lighthouse in the distance. Paint peels from its weathered siding like old scabs. Her grandfather's last known location before he vanished, just like the others.

Six mysterious disappearances in the past forty years, all connected to the lighthouse somehow.

Shaking slightly, Clara reached behind the hedge for the front door key, as instructed in the will. Bending at just the right angle to pull it out, her eyes caught something glinting in the overgrown garden – a brass compass, half-buried in the soil.

Clara's breath catches. In her grandfather's journal, he'd written about hiding a compass as a marker.

Find the key, find the compass.

When the needle spins, it points.

Dig deeper.

The compass needle whirls wildly as she picks it up. It points in the direction of the balcony and stops. Clara climbs up the steps, and as her feet land on the last step, the floorboards creak under her feet.

She stops suddenly; one sounds hollow. Her fingers find the edge, and the board lifts away easily.

There, she finds an old oilcloth. Clara lifts it out gently, unwrapping it to find another journal. The first entry makes her blood freeze:

The curse is real. Their names are whispers in the fog. They know, and now they're coming for me.

CHAPTER 2
THE HISTORIAN'S
WARNING

Clara stands at her upstairs window, watching the fog curl around the lighthouse in the distance. With the fog, she can only glimpse its white tower topped by a dark red roof, perched precariously on the cliff's edge where angry waves crash against the rocks below.

Even partially obscured, the massive structure draws her gaze like a lodestone.

Last night's discovery of her grandfather's hidden journal weighs heavy on her mind. The words continue to echo in her mind:

The curse is real.

The curse is real.

The curse is real.

The curse is real.

Clara wonders what he had found out that made him write those words. What curse had her grandfather been talking about?

She'd found some symbols in the journal, and Clara remembered seeing the same symbols in the newspaper clippings. The article said they always preceded another disappearance.

Once every seven years.

A knock at her door makes her jump.

"Breakfast is ready, dear!" Mrs. Thompson's cheerful voice carries through the wood, but she doesn't quite mask the undercurrent of strain. The shuffling footsteps from yesterday still haunt her thoughts—that grotesque parody of Mr. Thompson, with his vacant eyes and gray-tinged skin.

Then there's the odd-looking fellow that was following her. She still couldn't figure out what he wanted.

"Morning, Mildred. Coming!" Clara tucks the journal into her messenger bag alongside her tablet and recorder. If anyone in town knows anything about her grandfather's disappearance, she'll find them.

A place has been set in the dining room, the same delicate China as yesterday. Steam rises from a cup of coffee, and the scent of fresh scones fills the air. But Mrs. Thompson is nowhere to be seen.

Just as she eats the last of the strawberry-filled scone, Mrs. Thompson appears and begins clearing dishes. Her hands shake so badly that a cup clatters against its saucer.

"Are you alright?" Clara asks softly.

"Oh! Just fine, dear." Her smile is too bright, too fixed. "But if you're going out, stay away from the lighthouse. Especially in the fog. Terrible accidents happen there."

"What kind of accidents?"

Mrs. Thompson's face goes blank, like a curtain dropping. "I should check on the laundry." She hurries from the room, leaving Clara alone with the growing certainty that the entire town is hiding something.

Outside, the fog has thickened, transforming familiar buildings into looming shadows. Clara pulls out her grandfather's compass, watching the needle spin wildly before settling in a direction that can't possibly be north. Stuffing it back into her coat pocket, she heads toward the lighthouse, her footsteps echoing off wet cobblestones.

A few people hurry about their business, their faces practically buried in flannel or some thick cloth, their collars turned up against the fog and harsh cold.

Clara approaches an elderly man arranging crab traps outside *Fletcher's Fishing Supplies*.

"Excuse me," she begins. "I'm wondering if you knew Thomas Bennett?"

The man's weathered hands remain on the rope he's coiling. His eyes dart past her shoulder, then back down. "Can't help you, miss." He disappears into his shop, the bell jingling with finality as the door closes.

The same scene repeats at *The Rusty Anchor Pub*, where the morning bartender suddenly becomes engrossed in polishing already-gleaming glasses, and at the *Maritime Museum*, where the curator actually locks the door when she approaches.

"They won't talk to you." The voice comes from behind her, smooth as aged whiskey. Clara doesn't miss the edge of warning or the coolness of the tone.

She turns to find a man in his mid-thirties watching her from the shadow of a doorway.

Hair so golden they look like glittering coins falls across wire-rimmed glasses, and something about his intense gaze makes her journalist instincts prickle.

He steps forward, offering a tight smile that doesn't reach his eyes. Yet, Clara instantly notes how they sparkle like blue diamonds.

"Marcus Gale, town historian." He extends his hand.

His grip is firm and professional, but Clara notices how quickly he withdraws it.

What are you hiding?

"Clara Bennett. My grandfather passed and left me his cottage. I've come to look at it and maybe, learn a little about the reason for his sudden demise."

Something flickers across his face – Fear? "Reason? Do you think there was any special cause of his passing? Your grandfather was very old, you know."

"So you knew him then?"

Marcus holds Clara's gaze for a long moment, then lets out a small sigh. "Eldermere's charm is best appreciated from a distance." His tone is light, but there's a tone of warning beneath it. "Some stories aren't meant to be told."

Clara doesn't miss how he dodged her question. Unfazed, she doesn't look away. "What kind of stories then? Like why people have been disappearing every seven years and how the lighthouse might have something to do with it?"

Marcus's eyes narrow slightly. "I hope you're not planning to visit the lighthouse, Clara."

Even though her heart is racing one mile every second, she steps forward. "Should I not?" She forces her tone to remain cool, controlled.

"It's been closed for years. Structural concerns." He pulls a business card from his pocket and places it into her hand.

"If you're interested in Eldermere's history, come by the archives. I'll show you some of our... approved materials."

Clara doesn't miss the way he emphasizes 'approved'. She watches him leave, his footsteps eerily silent on the old pavement.

Clara hurries forward, the lighthouse coming into sight and disappearing as the fog moves.

The fog parts occasionally as Clara makes her way down Harbor Street, revealing glimpses of daily life that seem carefully staged. Children play hopscotch but their laughter sounds rehearsed. Shopkeepers arrange window displays with mechanical precision. Everyone smiles, nods, and keeps their eyes downcast.

The Maritime Museum catches her attention—specifically, the photographs in its window. Ships, crews, celebrations... but something's off. She moves closer, studying each image carefully. There, in every group photo, there are gaps where people should be standing, spaces that look deliberately left empty.

A plaque beneath one photo reads: *"Eldermere Harbor Master's Annual Gathering, 1975."* Clara counts seven conspicuous spaces in the group, like missing teeth in a forced smile.

The bell above the museum door chimes as she reaches for it. An elderly man emerges, locking the door before she can enter. "Closed for inventory," he mumbles, though Clara can see people inside through the window.

She's turning away when something catches her eye—a reflection in the glass. A figure watching her from across the street. She spins around, but they're gone. Yet, in the window's reflection, the shape remains like a glitch in reality.

There. Movement catches her eye. This time it's a real person, but not the same man from yesterday. He is more composed. More confident.

While the man from yesterday was shadowing her without really seeming like a threat, this man seems like he has a purpose. Could he hurt her?

She quickens her pace, her heart thundering against her ribs. As she throws a glance behind her, the fog parts briefly, revealing a flash of sandy hair and glasses.

Marcus.

Her journalistic instincts kick in. Clara rounds a corner sharply, pressing herself against the rough brick wall.

Footsteps approach, hesitate, then stop. She steps out, catching him mid-turn.

"Looking for someone?"

He doesn't even have the grace to look embarrassed. His eyes meet hers with confidence.

"It's my job to keep an eye on the town's interests."

"By stalking visitors?"

"By protecting them." He steps closer, his voice dropping. "Your grandfather didn't listen to warnings either. Look what happened to him."

Clara's breath catches. "I asked you if you knew him!"

"Everyone knew Thomas Bennett." Marcus's eyes dart to the lighthouse looming behind her. "Everyone knew what happened to him too."

Clara gasps. "Was he murdered?!"

"No." Marcus's face turns deathly white. The fear on his face is so palpable that Clara takes a step back. Marcus leans in and grabs her arm, his fingers tight enough to bruise.

"Clara, listen to me. Your grandfather was taken. Just like the others. Just like you will be if you don't leave Eldermere now."

She jerks free. "Is that a threat?"

"A prophecy." He backs away, fog curling around him like a shroud. "Some secrets protect themselves, Miss Bennett.

The lighthouse knows when someone gets too close to the truth."

Clara lets out a sharp gasp. "The curse. So it's true."

"Leave. For your own good." He melts into the mist, leaving Clara alone with her racing thoughts and the distant sound of waves crashing against the shore.

Above her, the lighthouse beacon pierces the fog like an accusing eye, watching, waiting.

Marcus's warning only proves she's on the right track. Clara squares her shoulders and starts walking.

The truth about Eldermere is hidden in that lighthouse. And she's going to find it, no matter what it costs.

But once at the lighthouse, Clara finds the entrance firmly sealed. Shaken by Marcus's words but undeterred, she decides to wait until it's dark to return and find another way in.

In the meantime, she decides to return to her grandfather's cottage.

"You knew some secrets, grandfather. Did you leave any more clues for me at the cottage? "

Marcus's warnings follow Clara as she makes her way back to her grandfather's cottage.

Inside, late morning light filters through dusty windows, catching motes that dance in the air. Clara moves from room to room, letting her fingers trail across furniture draped in white sheets.

There's something almost peaceful about the space in daylight—the worn leather armchair, the hooks by the door still holding her grandfather's old rain slicker, and the kettle on the stove that looks like it's waiting for someone to come home and make tea.

In the study, she finds a drawer that opens with a protesting creak. "What have we here?"

Among the yellowed papers and old receipts lies a small album bound in faded blue cloth. The first photo makes her sink into the nearby chair: herself at age three, birthday cake smeared across her face, her mother laughing in the background.

Another shows her first day of school, grip tight on her lunchbox, hair in uneven pigtails.

"How did you get these, old man?" she whispers to the empty room.

Beneath the photos, she finds letters in her mother's familiar handwriting, dated through the years:

Dear Dad,

Clara lost her first tooth today. She was so proud, showing everyone at the grocery store. Sometimes when she smiles, she looks just like you...

Dear Dad,

It's the first day of middle school. She's already talking about becoming a journalist. Remember how I used to steal your notepads to write my own newspaper articles? That investigative spirit must run in our blood...

Clara's hands tremble as she reads. Every milestone, every triumph and setback, carefully documented and sent to a grandfather she never knew existed.

Why had her mother kept him secret? Why had she never mentioned these letters?

The last one is dated just months before her mother's death:

Dear Dad,

I know you think you're protecting us by keeping us away, but Clara's old enough now. Whatever darkness you're investigating in Eldermere, whatever danger you think might follow you – she deserves to know her family. Her heritage. Please consider...

The letter ends there, unfinished. Clara wipes moisture from her cheeks, unsure when she started crying.

She spends the rest of the morning piecing together fragments of a relationship she never knew existed, watching the sun arc across the sky.

But as shadows lengthen across the floorboards, her thoughts return to the lighthouse.

Her grandfather had been investigating something in Eldermere – something dangerous enough to keep him from his family. Something that eventually led to his sudden death.

As twilight approaches, Clara tucks the album and letters carefully into her bag alongside the journal.

Whatever secrets the lighthouse holds, she's going to uncover them. For her grandfather. For her mother. For all the questions she never got to ask.

***

Clara approaches the lighthouse; her footsteps muffled by the damp cobblestones.

Her heart thunders against her ribs as she walks around it until she spots what she's been looking for – an ancient drainage pipe running up the lighthouse's weathered side.

Near its base, barely visible in the gloom, a maintenance hatch hangs slightly ajar. Clara tests the pipe with her weight. It groans but holds.

The metal is slick with moisture, and her hands tremble as she begins to climb. One wrong move, one slip, and she'll plummet to the rocks below.

The fog swirls around her, thick enough to mask her from anyone watching but thin enough to reveal the dizzying height as she ascends. Each foot up feels like a small eternity.

The pipe creaks ominously. Finally, her fingers brush the hatch. It takes all her strength to pry it open wider. The rusted hinges protest with a sound that seems to echo across the entire harbor.

Clara pulls herself through the opening, dropping quietly onto a narrow maintenance platform.

The lighthouse's interior is pitch black except for thin slivers of light from the beacon above, rotating with mechanical precision. The air inside is different—heavy, ancient, tasting of salt and the sea.

The spiral staircase stretches above her like a twisted spine. Her flashlight beam catches dust motes dancing in the air, swirling in patterns that seem almost deliberate.

As she begins to climb, her footsteps echo strangely, making the space seem larger than it is.

That's when she hears them – whispers, too faint to make out words but clearly voices, seemingly coming from the very walls.

They rise and fall like waves, growing louder as she ascends. Clara's grip tightens on the railing, her knuckles white.

Halfway up, she freezes. There, at the next landing, a figure stands in the darkness.

The beacon's light passes through it, revealing a translucent form she knows all too well from photographs – her grandfather.

His eyes lock with hers, filled with an urgency that makes her blood run cold.

One spectral hand reaches toward her, beckoning her upward before the figure fades into nothing.

Clara's legs threaten to give out. Every instinct screams at her to run, to flee back down the stairs and never return.

But she forces herself to take another step up, then another. Her grandfather was trying to tell her something. The answers she seeks must be near.

Near the top, something catches her eye – a scrap of dark fabric snagged on a protruding nail, gently swaying in a breeze she can't feel.

The cloth is still damp, recently torn. Someone else has been here recently enough that the evidence hasn't had time to dry.

The whispers grow louder, more insistent. Clara pulls the fabric free, studying it in her flashlight's beam.

The material is expensive, well-made. Her mind races through possibilities – Marcus's coat had been similar, but she'd seen others in town wearing dark clothing.

Is this connected to her grandfather's disappearance? To the figure that had been following her? How was Marcus involved in all of this? He seemed the most anxious to get rid of her.

Above her, the beacon's light stutters, plunging the stairwell into total darkness for a heartbeat.

When it returns, Clara swears she sees multiple shadows moving on the walls – shadows that don't match her own movements.

She's not alone in the lighthouse.

And whatever's up there with her, it knows she's here.

CHAPTER 3
UNVEILING
THE CURSE

Clara's flashlight beam catches something on the wall as she reaches the top landing—her heart nearly stops. Dozens of nautical maps cover every surface, their edges curling with age and moisture.

Red strings connect various points, all culminating at the lighthouse. Beneath each string, dates are scrawled in different hands: 1887, 1894, 1901...every seven years, like clockwork.

Her hands trembling, she moves closer. Intricate drawings cover the spaces between maps— symbols she recognizes from her grandfather's journal.

They seem to writhe in her flashlight's beam as if alive. One depicts the lighthouse surrounded by twisted faces in the fog, their mouths open in silent screams.

"Oh God, Grandpa," she whispers, touching a familiar scrawl in the margin. "You were trying to warn them."

The beacon's light sweeps through the room, illuminating a final drawing that makes her blood freeze—a detailed illustration of the lighthouse acting as a beacon not for ships but for something else—something that lured people to their doom.

A sudden gust of wind passes, and then her flashlight flickers and goes off. In the darkness, she hears it— ragged breathing that isn't her own.

The beacon sweeps around again, and Clara screams. A figure stands between her and the stairs— grey skin stretched tight over an almost skeletal face, empty eye sockets gleaming with an otherworldly light. Its mouth opens impossibly wide, revealing rows of needle-like teeth.

Clara bolts for the stairs, her foot catching on the top step. She tumbles down several steps before catching herself on the railing. Behind her, something scrapes against the walls— coming closer.

She half-runs, half-stumbles down the spiral staircase, her shoulder slamming into the curved wall.

The thing above her moves faster than should be possible, its ragged breathing echoing off the walls.

Clara reaches the bottom, lunging for the door. The handle won't turn. "No, no, no!" She throws her weight against it, but it doesn't budge. The scraping sounds grow closer.

Desperate, she backs up and kicks with all her strength. Once. Twice. The door groans. Behind her, fetid breath washes over her neck. With a scream of pure terror, she kicks again.

The door bursts open, and Clara tumbles out into the fog, gasping in great lungfuls of clean air as she scrambles away from the lighthouse.

She doesn't stop running until she's several yards away. When she finally turns back, the lighthouse stands silent and dark, as if nothing had happened.

But Clara knows what she saw. And she knows why her grandfather's final journal entry had been written in such a shaky hand.

Some things, once seen, can never be unseen.

Through the fog's ghostly tendrils, Clara catches movement—a shadow darker than the rest, watching from behind a stack of weathered crates.

Her terror transforms into white-hot anger. After what she'd just experienced, she's done with being afraid.

"Hey!" She charges forward, her boots pounding against the wet cobblestones. The figure turns to flee, but Clara's newfound rage makes her faster.

"Stop right there!"

She rounds the corner just in time to see him stumble. The man's shoulder catches a lamppost, spinning him around.

The foggy lamplight illuminates a familiar face—the strange man who'd followed her that yesterday.

Clara's hand shoots out, grabbing his sleeve. The fabric tears slightly, and her breath catches. The material is identical to the scrap she'd found in the lighthouse.

"It was you," she snarls, shoving him against the lamppost. "You've been playing games, haven't you? Skulking around in the lighthouse, trying to scare me away?"

Oliver's eyes are wide with genuine fear. "No, you don't understand—"

"What's not to understand?" Clara pulls the torn piece from her pocket, holding it against his shirt. "Perfect match. Did you think it was funny, pretending to be some kind of monster? Terrorizing people who get too close to the truth? What's your name and why are you doing this?"

He grabs her wrist, his grip surprisingly gentle despite his panic. "My name is Oliver. Listen to me. What you saw in there— that wasn't me. I've been trying to protect you."

What is it with the people in this town and protecting visitors? "Protect me?" Clara laughs bitterly. "By stalking me? By playing ghost?"

"The real ghosts are far worse." His voice drops to a whisper, eyes darting to the shadows around them. "I've seen them too. They're drawn to people who dig too deep, who ask too many questions. People like your grandfather."

A chill runs down Clara's spine, but she maintains her grip. "How do you know about my grandfather?"

"Because I tried to warn him too." Oliver's face contorts with what looks like genuine anguish. "But he wouldn't listen. Just like you won't listen. The lighthouse... it has a hunger that can't be satisfied. And you're making yourself a target."

"You're insane," Clara says, but her voice wavers.

"The torn shirt?" Oliver's laugh holds no humor. "I was up there, trying to... to stop it. But you can't stop what lives in that place. You can only try to keep others away from it."

A distant fog horn blares, making them both jump. Oliver uses the momentary distraction to wrench free from her grasp.

"Please," he calls over his shoulder as he backs away. "Go home. Leave Eldermere. Before you become another whisper in the fog."

He turns and runs, disappearing into the mist before Clara can stop him. She's left holding a scrap of fabric, her certainty crumbling like sand between her fingers.

The terror she'd felt in the lighthouse had been real—too real for any human trick. If this man wasn't behind what she'd seen in the lighthouse...

The beacon sweeps across the fog above her, and Clara swears she can hear whispers in its light—countless voices, all crying out in warning.

Clara walks slowly back through the fog-shrouded streets, her mind racing faster than her feet can carry her. The torn fabric weighs heavy in her pocket, like a piece of evidence that proves everything and nothing at once.

The fear in Oliver's eyes had seemed genuine— too raw to be fabricated. But in Eldermere, she's learning that nothing is quite what it seems. The friendly smiles of townspeople mask dark secrets. Even the fog itself feels like a conspirator, helping to hide decades of lies and disappeared souls.

She pauses at the harbor's edge, watching the lighthouse's beam cut through the mist. Each sweep of light seems to reveal another layer of mystery: her grandfather's cryptic warnings, Marcus's veiled threats, Oliver's desperate attempts to... what? Save her? Or lead her deeper into danger?

The thing she'd seen in the lighthouse tower flashes through her mind— those empty eye sockets, that impossible mouth.

If Oliver had been trying to scare her away, why risk his own life climbing up there? And if he wasn't behind it, then what had she actually encountered?

Her journalist's mind tries to arrange the pieces: seven-year cycles of disappearances, a town bound by silence, and supernatural encounters that feel too real to dismiss.

But every answer she uncovers only leads to more questions, spreading like cracks in ice.

The foghorn sounds again, mournful and warning. Clara wraps her arms around herself, suddenly chilled to the bone. Whether Oliver is friend or foe, one thing is becoming terrifyingly clear— she's stirring up something.

***

By the time she reaches Mrs. Thompson's B&B, her legs are trembling from exhaustion. The warmth inside should feel welcoming, but even here, shadows seem to lurk in every corner. Clara climbs the stairs, her footsteps echoing in the empty hallway.

She's reaching for her door handle when she sees it— a cream-colored envelope on the floor, pushed just far enough under her door to be noticeable. Her name is written in an elegant, old-fashioned script she hasn't seen before.

With shaking fingers, Clara tears it open. The paper inside holds just one sentence, written in deep red ink that looks disturbingly like dried blood:

"Leave Eldermere before you become the next lost soul."

The paper slips from her numb fingers, floating to the floor like a fallen leaf. Above her, the floorboards creak— but when Clara looks up, the hallway is empty.

Empty, except for the shadows that seem to be watching, waiting, growing longer with each passing second.

CHAPTER 4

SECRETS IN THE FOG

The thick fog often shrouds the town, adding to the sense of mystery, but tonight, it felt almost alive, swirling with unseen intentions.

Clara watches it curl against her window, forming shapes that disappear the moment she tries to focus on them.

The threatening note from last night sits on her bedside table, its blood-red ink a stark reminder that time might be running out.

There's one person that may be able to give her answers.

Clara tells Mrs. Thompson she will skip breakfast and heads out. The crisp morning air brings little relief from the oppressive atmosphere.

The archives building looms before her, its Victorian architecture somehow more menacing than grand in the perpetual haze. Clara straightens her shoulders and pushes through the heavy oak doors.

The scent of old paper and leather bindings fills her nose as she enters. Marcus stands behind the counter, bent over a leather-bound volume.

His fair hair falls across his eyes as he reads, and Clara finds herself noticing how his tall, lean frame fills out his well-cut clothes. His refined looks would fit somewhere posh or in a university library than this haunted town.

Then, as though he senses she's staring at him, he looks up. Something in his steel-blue eyes makes her pulse quicken— and not in a pleasant way.

Clara approaches the counter, her footsteps echoing in the hushed space. A document lies open before Marcus. She steals a glance at it, and her heart stutters.

The elegant, flowing script perfectly matches the threatening note.

"You wrote it, didn't you?" She pulls the note from her bag, slapping it on the counter between them. "Was this supposed to scare me away?"

Marcus doesn't even glance at the paper. "I don't know what you're talking about."

"Don't lie to me." Clara leans forward, lowering her voice. "I need access to the town records. The real ones, not whatever sanitized version you show to tourists."

"Those records are restricted." His jaw tightens. "Town council policy."

"My grandfather disappeared here. I have a right to know what happened to him."

A muscle ticks in Marcus's cheek. "Or maybe you're just looking for your next big story? Small town secrets make compelling headlines, don't they?"

Clara feels her face flush. "Yes, I'm a journalist. And yes, this could be a story. But this is also about my family— about finding the truth."

"The truth?" Marcus's laugh holds no humor. "Sometimes the truth is better left buried, Clara."

He turns away, disappearing into the stacks. When he returns, he's carrying a worn book about Eldermere's maritime history. "Here. This should satisfy your curiosity."

Clara flips through the pages, immediately recognizing the useless propaganda. But then something catches her eye— a detailed drawing of tunnels beneath the town, their winding paths resembling the tentacles of some ancient creature.

While Marcus busies himself with reorganizing some files, she quickly snaps several photos with her phone.

"Find anything interesting?" His voice makes her jump. Marcus stands closer now, his eyes boring into hers with an intensity that makes her skin prickle. "You should know, Clara— too much curiosity can be dangerous in Eldermere. Worse things have happened to people for less."

The threat hangs in the air between them. Clara forces herself to hold his gaze, even as her heart hammers against her ribs. "Is that what happened to my grandfather? He was too curious?"

Something flickers across Marcus's face—pain? Regret? But it's gone before she can be sure. "Good day, Miss Bennett."

Clara notes the sudden formal use of her name. Grabbing her coat, Clara heads back to the B&B to find Mrs. Thompson anxiously polishing already-gleaming silverware.

When Clara mentions Marcus and the tunnels, the older woman's hands still.

"They say they connect to the lighthouse," Mrs. Thompson whispers, her eyes darting to the windows. "But some places in this town weren't meant to be explored." She hesitates, then adds, "And Clara? Stay away from Marcus Gale. Some people in this town... they carry darkness where ever they go."

"What do you mean?"

But Mrs. Thompson just shakes her head, returning to her furious polishing, leaving Clara alone with her mounting questions and the growing certainty that everyone in this town knows far more than they're willing to say.

Frustrated by half-truths and warnings, Clara heads toward the tunnels but stops short.

Something pulls her toward her grandfather's cottage instead— intuition or perhaps something more supernatural, guiding her steps through the swirling fog.

Inside the cottage, Clara follows a hunch and runs her fingers along the study's wood paneling, remembering how her grandfather's journal mentioned hidden spaces.

A hollow sound makes her pause. Heart racing, she presses harder, and a panel swings inward with a groan of ancient hinges.

"Oh my God," she whispers.

A small chamber lies beyond, smelling of dust and secrets. Clara's flashlight beam reveals shelves lined with leather-bound journals and ledgers, their spines dated back to the 1800s.

She pulls one down with trembling fingers, and names spill from its pages—dozens of them, each accompanied by dates and locations of disappearances.

"Elizabeth Marie Gale, vanished near the lighthouse, October 1887..."

"James Harrison, last seen entering the fog, March 1894..."

"Samuel Caldwell, disappeared from the harbor, July 1901..."

The dates follow the seven-year pattern she'd noticed before until exactly 7 years ago. If this is correct, someone is due to disappear soon.

But it's the photographs that make her blood run cold. Sepia-toned images spread before her like a macabre timeline. In the first, dated 1980, a group stands before the lighthouse—including her grandfather, looking much younger but unmistakable.

Each subsequent photo shows fewer people, faces vanishing one by one until only three remain in the final shot. Her grandfather stands at the edge, his expression haunted, as if he knows he'll be next.

"No, no, no," Clara mutters, diving deeper into the documents.

Letters emerge, yellowed and crisp with age. The handwriting varies, but the message remains consistent: *"The necessary sacrifices must continue."*

"The town's safety depends on our silence."

"The pattern must be maintained."

One letter, dated just months before her grandfather's disappearance, bears a signature that makes her gasp: *"With grave concern, Edmund Gale."*

"Could that be Marcus's father?" she breathes. Maybe his family has something to do with this; that's why Mrs. Thompson warned her about him.

An old map of Eldermere falls from between the pages. Red marks dot its surface, each indicating a disappearance.

When connected, they form a spiral pattern, centering on the lighthouse like a twisted constellation.

At the bottom of the pile, newspaper clippings tell sanitized versions of the truth.

"Local Man Missing, Presumed Drowned."

"Tourist Disappears in Fog."

"Search Called Off for Missing Historian."

Black lines strike through key details, but her grandfather's neat handwriting fills the margins with questions:

"Why no body recovered?"

"Witness reports excluded"

"Connection to 1894 incident?"

"They're hiding the pattern"

Clara sits back on her heels, her mind reeling. The truth she's uncovered is worse than anything she imagined. Not just random disappearances but calculated sacrifices.

Not just a curse, but a conspiracy spanning generations. And Marcus— is he just another link in this chain of darkness, or something more?

She's alone in this. Oliver might be trying to help, but he's clearly terrified. Mrs. Thompson knows more than she's saying, but she's trapped by her own fears. And Marcus... Marcus could be her greatest enemy.

The fog presses against the windows, thicker than ever, as if trying to peer in at her discoveries. Clara begins gathering the most important documents, knowing she needs proof before confronting anyone with what she's learned.

A floorboard creaks lightly.

"Hello?" Clara calls out, her voice shaking. "Is someone there?"

She turns toward the door just as a shadow fills it. Before she can scream, powerful hands shove her backward.

Clara catches a glimpse of a face she's seen just as she hits the ground.

Clara scrambles to her feet, her heart hammering against her ribs. She catches only a glimpse of her attacker. It is the man who had taken her to Mrs. Thompson's Cottage on that first night.

His features are twisted with fury— before he vanishes into the fog that seems to reach in for him like a living thing.

CHAPTER 5

UNMASKING THE FACADE

The dense fog seemed to seep into Clara's mind, clouding her trust as she realized that danger lurks around every corner.

The evidence from her grandfather's cottage weighs heavy in her bag, each step carrying her further into the darkness that had claimed so many others.

Her feet move of their own accord, drawn inexorably toward the lighthouse. Its beam cuts through the mist like an accusing finger, pointing out secrets better left buried.

Perhaps there, in that towering structure, she'll find the connection between her grandfather's research and his fate.

The sound comes first—footsteps on wet cobblestones, too measured to be casual.

Clara's pulse quickens as she recognizes the deliberate pace. Did her attacker from the cottage follow her or was it someone else?

She breaks into a run, but the fog plays tricks with direction. The lighthouse appears and disappears in the mist, seemingly shifting position with each glimpse.

Behind her, the footsteps quicken.

A hand grabs for her coat—she feels the brush of fingers against wool. Clara spins away, but her heel catches on the uneven ground.

She stumbles, the world tilting—

A shadow bursts from the fog. For a moment, Clara sees the same cold fury in her attacker's eyes that she'd glimpsed at the cottage.

But before he can reach her, another figure barrels into him with shocking force.

The two men grapple in the mist, their shapes distorting like smoke. Her attacker throws a punch that misses, then suddenly stops.

Something in the fog seems to call to him. He backs away, his face a mask of frustration and fear, before the mist swallows him whole.

Clara's rescuer straightens, turning toward her. In the lighthouse's sweeping beam, she recognizes the strange man who's been following her—Oliver, the one who'd warned her at the lighthouse before.

"Are you hurt?" His voice is gentler than she expected, filled with genuine concern.

"Who are you? Really?" Clara demands, though her voice shakes.

He offers his hand, helping her up. "I told you I've been trying to protect you since you arrived in Eldermere, though you've made it remarkably difficult."

Pain flashes across Oliver's face. "Clara, they aren't joking around. You need to leave. Tonight. Before you become another name in those ledgers you found."

Clara's blood runs cold. "How did you—"

"Because I've been watching. Trying to prevent history from repeating itself." He grips her shoulders, his touch urgent but careful. "This town isn't safe for you. Please. Don't let your grandfather's fate become your own."

The lighthouse beam sweeps across them, and for a moment, Clara swears she sees something in Oliver's eyes— a depth of knowledge and fear that makes her own terror seem shallow in comparison. He's seen something in this town, something that haunts him still.

But before she can ask more questions, he steps back, melting into the fog like all the others, leaving Clara alone with the weight of his warning and the growing certainty that she's stumbled into something far darker than she ever imagined.

Clara's footsteps echo through Mrs. Thompson's front hall, mingling with those of a man hurrying out the door. Something about his silhouette tugs at her memory, but he disappears into the fog before she can place him.

Inside, she finds Mrs. Thompson trembling.

"Mrs. Thompson! What's going on? Are you alright?"

"Fine, fine." She won't meet Clara's eyes. "Would you like some tea? I just baked scones—"

"The lighthouse," Clara interrupts. "Something happened there, didn't it? Something you're all trying to hide?"

The teacup in Mrs. Thompson's hands clatters against its saucer. "Such terrible fog today. They say it might rain— But my dear, you have to leave. What happened to George. Oh Clara, take your things and run. Never return here. Never look back."

Clara watches her nervous movements, seeing how even those who've shown her kindness are bound by the town's secrets.

But she wasn't going to cower away or be bullied into leaving.

***

The bell above the archives' door chimes as Clara enters. Marcus stands at his usual post, but something about his posture suggests he's been waiting for her.

"What's in the lighthouse?" Clara demands without preamble. "What are you all trying so hard to hide?"

"Miss Bennett—"

"Cut it out with the formal address and no more deflections." She steps closer. "Someone just tried to attack me. Twice. And somehow, I don't think they were acting alone."

Marcus's jaw tightens. "I've told you to leave this alone."

"Prove you're not involved." Clara lifts her chin. "Come to the lighthouse with me."

"Absolutely not." His voice turns harsh. "I've stayed alive by staying away from that place, and everyone involved. I keep my lips shut!"

"Like your ancestors did?" Clara pulls out one of the letters she'd found. "Edmund Gale—that was your father, wasn't it? He knew about the disappearances. He was part of it."

Marcus moves so quickly she barely registers it. His fingers wrap around her elbow, pulling her toward the back of the archives.

But instead of fear, Clara feels electricity shoot through her at his touch.

"You have no idea what you're dealing with," he growls, pushing her into a shadowy alcove. "My father, my grandfather— they all tried to protect this town's secrets. And they all paid the price. George, Mrs. Thompson's son. He was one of the disappearances."

Clara lets out a shaky breath. Mrs. Thompson's son. That's why she's so frightened. That's why she asked her to leave.

Shock knocks Clara backwards until she hits a bookshelf. Marcus looms over her, his breath coming quick and shallow. "And now you're diving headfirst into the same darkness that took them."

"Then help me, Marcus." Her voice softens. This close, she can see flecks of gray in his blue eyes, can almost touch his full apple shaped lips.

The air between them charges with something beyond fear or anger. Marcus's gaze drops to her lips, and Clara's breath catches. She feels herself swaying forward—

CRASH!

They spring apart as one of the side windows explodes inward, sending glass skittering across the floor. Marcus rushes to investigate while Clara presses a hand to her thundering heart.

When he returns, something has shifted in his expression.

"My great-grandmother was the first," he says quietly. "She discovered something in the lighthouse— something that changed her. When she tried to warn others, she vanished. Just like my grandfather did, and then my father when he was trying to find out what happened to my grandfather." His voice breaks. "Just like everyone who gets too close to the truth."

Clara sees it now—the pain behind his warnings, the weight of generations of loss.

"Let me walk you back," Marcus says suddenly. "It's getting dark."

Outside, the fog has grown impossibly thick, pressing against them like a living thing. Clara can barely see her own feet on the cobblestones.

Marcus takes her arm, guiding her by memory through the ghostly white void.

"Come on. It'll be alright. I know this town like the back of my hands. I'll take you through a short cut," he murmurs.

The sound comes out of nowhere— an engine roaring to life, headlights suddenly burning through the fog like demon eyes. Clara freezes, but Marcus moves instantly, shoving her hard to the side.

They roll together, the car's rush of air barely missing them. But their momentum carries them too far. Clara feels empty air beneath her, and realizes they've reached a cliff's edge. The ground crumbles.

She screams as she starts to fall, but Marcus's hand shoots out, catching her wrist. Clara dangles over the abyss, waves crashing against rocks far below, while Marcus strains to hold her.

"Don't let go," she gasps.

"Never," he promises through gritted teeth. He gives a firm swing, and Clara is lifted over his head and thrown onto firm ground.

They both lay on the ground, relief making them too weak to move.

Above them, footsteps crunch on gravel, approaching slowly through the fog.

CHAPTER 6
CONFRONTATION AT THE LIGHTHOUSE

A figure emerges from the fog— a weathered face twisted with an expression filled with hatred. Clara feels her heart race. It's the man who shoved her.

Marcus and Clara scramble to their feet. Marcus shoves Clara behind him.

He comes close until his face is mere inches from Marcus's. He jabs a finger at his face. "You shouldn't have interfered, son." His voice is thick and cold.

"Henry, no. No more hurting innocent people," Marcus yells.

"You know we don't have a choice. This is our way here."

Before Marcus can respond, Henry lunges forward with surprising speed for a man his age.

His fist connects with Marcus's jaw, sending him staggering.

"What are you doing?" Marcus spits blood onto the gravel. "Henry, you've known me since I was—"

"Exactly why I'm surprised at your foolishness. When they choose to come, they become responsible for whatever happens to them!"

Henry swings again, but this time Marcus is ready. He blocks the punch and grapples with the older man, both of them struggling in the mist.

Clara scrambles to her feet, shouting, "Stop it!" Clara looks around for something to hit Henry with.

But he suddenly breaks free of Marcus's grip, backing away. His chest heaves as he looks between them, something like grief crossing his features.

"The stranger," he says, gesturing to Clara. The lighthouse brought her. She has a purpose here, just like her grandfather did, just like yours did, Marcus. Don't you see? It has to be fulfilled."

"By getting her killed?" Marcus advances, but Henry holds up his hands.

"You can't fight what's coming with fists, boy." Henry's voice softens. "Some debts can only be paid one way. Stop intefering in what cannot be stopped. She chose to start this, let her finish it."

Henry turns and walks into the fog, his silhouette dissolving like smoke. The sound of his footsteps fades until only the distant crash of waves remains.

Marcus holds Clara's hand, his own trembling. "We need to get out of here. Now."

But Clara grips his arm with her other hand. "No. It has to end, Marcus. At the lighthouse."

"You don't understand what's up there," he says, looking toward the distant beam cutting through the darkness.

"I went there as a kid. What I saw—" He shudders. "I still have nightmares."

"I've seen them too," Clara whispers. "The shadows that aren't shadows. The faces in the windows. But think about it,

Marcus. Seven years. That's the pattern, isn't it? If we don't end this now, who's next? You? Me? Another innocent person?"

She takes his face in her hands, forcing him to look at her. "Your father couldn't do it. Your grandfather couldn't. My grandfather tried and failed. But we're here now, together. We have to try."

Marcus stares at the lighthouse, its beam seeming to pause on them for a moment, as if in recognition. It takes a long moment, but finally he nods. "Together then."

***

The beam cuts through the darkness with mechanical precision, but tonight its light seems different, more urgent, as if it too knows what's coming.

"We don't have to do this," Marcus says, his voice rough with concern. They stand at the lighthouse's base, waves crashing against the rocks below.

After pulling her from the cliff's edge, something has shifted between them—trust born of shared danger.

Clara takes his hand. "Your family and mine have sacrificed enough. We have to end it."

"The legends say no one who enters on a night like this ever returns."

"Then we'll be the first."

The door groans open at Clara's touch, as if inviting them in. The beam sweeps overhead, casting strange shadows that dance across the walls. Each step up the spiral staircase echoes with memories of her last terrifying visit.

"Clara."

The whispered voice stops her cold. Marcus tenses beside her.

"You hear it too?" she breathes.

A figure materializes in the darkness ahead— her grandfather, his form translucent but clearer than she's ever seen him. His eyes hold a desperate urgency.

"Follow," he mouths, turning toward a section of the wall that appears solid.

Clara moves forward, drawn by an instinct she can't explain. Her fingers find a hidden catch, and a panel swings inward, revealing a narrow passage descending into darkness.

"The original lighthouse plans never showed this," Marcus whispers.

They follow the ghost down crude stone steps, the air growing thick with age and secrets. The passage opens into a chamber that must lie directly beneath the lighthouse's foundation.

Their flashlight beams reveal walls covered in strange symbols—similar to those from her grandfather's journal but older and cruder.

Her grandfather's spirit points to a particular section of the wall. As Clara approaches, the symbols begin to glow with a faint, phosphorescent light.

"My God," Marcus breathes, running his fingers over the glowing marks. "These are records."

The symbols twist and shift before Clara's eyes, forming images that play across the wall like a primitive film.

She sees a ship breaking apart in a storm, desperate sailors clinging to debris, and the town's founders appearing on the beach, not to help but to wait.

"No," she whispers as the truth unfolds before them.

The founders murdered the shipwrecked sailors, stealing their charts and the precious cargo they'd managed to save.

But one survivor remained— a shaman, mortally wounded but not yet dead. As his blood soaked into the shore, he raised his hands toward the sky.

The images show fog pouring from his lips with his final breath, enveloping the town.

The founders tried to flee, but the mist followed them, whispering with the voices of the betrayed. The curse had begun.

"The town's guilt made manifest," Marcus says softly. "The fog isn't just horrible weather— it's the souls of those murdered sailors, demanding justice."

"And the disappearances?" Clara's voice shakes.

Her grandfather's spirit nods sadly, pointing to more symbols. Every seven years, the curse demands retribution— a soul for each sailor betrayed.

The founders made a dark bargain, choosing sacrifices to appease the curse and keep the town safe. Those who threatened to expose the truth were the first to be marked.

"That's why they took my father," Marcus whispers. "Why they took your grandfather. They were getting too close."

"And now?" Clara turns to her grandfather's ghost.

His expression is grave as he points to the final symbols— a warning that the cycle must continue until the curse is broken or until the fog claims every soul in Eldermere.

A sudden chill sweeps through the chamber. Above them, footsteps echo on the lighthouse stairs— many footsteps, moving with dreadful purpose.

At first, Clara thinks they are ghosts until she realizes they're real human footsteps. They are no longer alone.

More symbols illuminate across the chamber walls, revealing the terrible bargain that followed the curse. Clara watches as generations of town leaders— faces she recognizes from old photographs— gather in secret, choosing who will be sacrificed next. The fog whispers grow louder as if the very memories fuel their anger.

"The pact," Marcus says, his voice hollow. "They convinced themselves it was necessary. Seven years of peace in exchange for one life."

Clara's grandfather's spirit points to a particular scene unfolding on the wall—a recent meeting. Clara and Marcus look at the faces gathered around a table, passing a leather-bound book between them.

"I know these men from town. The ledger," Marcus gasps. "They were choosing their next victim."

It takes him a moment to recollect himself. "My father refused to participate." Marcus's hand finds hers in the darkness. "That's why they chose him. Just like they chose your grandfather when he discovered too much."

The ghost nods solemnly. The walls show one final vision— the curse can only be broken by exposing the truth, by ending the cycle of sacrifice that has only fed the darkness for generations.

Heavy footsteps echo from above.

"They're here," Marcus whispers.

Shadows appear in the passage doorway. Henry steps into the chamber first, his face now clearly visible in the glowing light. Behind him, several townspeople file in, their expressions grim.

"Miss Bennett." His voice is cold as the fog itself. "You should have heeded our warnings."

Clara stands her ground. "Henry. I know you're the one who's been coordinating the sacrifices."

"To protect this town." Henry's eyes gleam with zealous conviction. "Just as my father did, and his father before him. The curse must be appeased."

"The curse grows stronger with each sacrifice," Marcus counters. "You're not protecting anyone— you're feeding the darkness."

"And you." Henry turns to Marcus with disgust. "Your father died because he was weak. Because he couldn't understand the necessity of our actions. I had hoped you would show more wisdom."

Clara feels Marcus tense beside her. "My father died because he had the courage to stand against this madness."

"The truth has to come out," Clara says. "Look at what this secret has done to all of you. The fear, the guilt— it's destroying this town more surely than any curse."

"The truth?" Henry laughs bitterly. "The truth is that we've kept this town safe for generations. And we'll continue to do so, no matter the cost."

The townspeople move to encircle them, the exit now completely blocked. Clara feels Marcus step closer, his shoulder brushing hers. In that touch, she feels his silent support, his determination to face whatever comes next together.

Her grandfather's spirit watches from the corner, his form growing fainter as the confrontation builds.

But his final lines in the journal burn in Clara's mind: *only the truth can break the curse.* Only by exposing the darkness to light can Eldermere ever truly be free.

Clara squares her shoulders, facing the advancing townspeople. The slow-burning attraction she's felt for Marcus has crystallized in this moment of crisis into something stronger—trust, partnership, the certainty that together they can end this nightmare.

"You've all been wrong," she says, her voice gaining strength. "Every sacrifice, every secret, every life taken—it's only made the curse stronger. The fog grows thicker, the whispers louder. Can't you see? The only way to end this is to stop feeding it."

The glowing symbols pulse on the walls, casting eerie shadows across determined faces. The air grows thick with tension and centuries of guilt.

Henry steps forward, something dark glinting in his hand. "Then you leave us no choice."

Behind him, the fog begins to seep into the chamber, curling around their feet like hungry serpents.

The lighthouse trembles, ancient stone groaning like a living thing. The fog pours through every crack and crevice, but this time, it's different— thicker, alive with evil purpose. It coils around their ankles like spectral chains.

"You should have heeded the warnings, Clara." The man's eyes reflect the otherworldly glow as he steps forward. "Now you've left us no choice."

The fog surges suddenly, knocking Clara and Marcus off their feet and pinning them against the wall with an impossible force.

Around them, the townspeople's faces distort in the pulsing light, their features transforming into something inhuman.

"The curse..." Marcus gasps, struggling against the fog's grip. "It's taking control of them."

The leader raises a ceremonial dagger, its blade inscribed with familiar symbols. "The sacrifice must be made. The cycle must continue."

Clara watches in horror as the townspeople advance, their movements jerky and unnatural.

The fog thickens until she can barely see Marcus beside her. His hand finds hers in the darkness.

"I'm sorry," she whispers.

The dagger catches the light. The fog writhes with anticipation. This is how it ends— not with redemption, but with darkness claiming two more victims.

A voice cuts through the chaos: "STOP!"

Oliver bursts into the chamber, but the fog slams him back against the wall too.

He struggles forward, each step a battle against the supernatural force. In his hand, something glints—a medallion covered in ancient markings.

"The shaman's talisman," the leader hisses. "Where did you—"

"I found it," Oliver gasps, "in the caves. Been searching... for months." His eyes meet Clara's. "There's still a way... to end this."

He pushes forward another step, but the fog constricts around him like a python. Blood trickles from his nose with the effort of resisting its power.

"The curse demands payment," the leader says. "Blood for blood. Death for death."

"No." Oliver's voice strengthens. "It demands justice. Atonement. A willing sacrifice to break the chain of forced ones."

The fog pulses, as if considering his words. The pressure on Clara's chest lessens slightly.

"My family helped start this," Oliver continues. "We were there that night, when the sailors were betrayed. Their blood is on our hands." He raises the medallion. "I offer myself, freely, to end it."

"Oliver, don't—" Clara starts, but he's already moving.

The fog suddenly releases them, sending everyone stumbling. Oliver runs for the stairs, taking them two at a time toward the lighthouse's peak.

Clara and Marcus chase after him, but the fog swirls between them, slowing their pursuit.

They emerge onto the top platform just as Oliver reaches the railing. The storm that's been building breaks overhead, lightning illuminating his face in stark burst.

"Oliver, please!" Clara reaches for him. "There has to be another way!"

But she sees in his eyes that his decision is made. The medallion begins to glow with an inner light, responding to his intent.

"The curse can only be broken by willing sacrifice," he says, voice carrying over the wind. "By someone choosing to pay the price of our ancestors' sins." He looks at Clara and Marcus. "Live. Tell our story. Make it mean something."

"Oliver—"

"Spirits of the mist and sea," he raises the medallion high, "I offer myself in payment for our wrongs. Accept this atonement and end this cycle of death!"

Lightning splits the sky. The medallion flares like a captured star

And Oliver steps backwards into empty air.

Clara's scream is lost in the explosion of light that follows. The shockwave knocks everyone to the ground. The fog surges upward like a tidal wave, then—impossibly—begins to dissolve.

Through tears, Clara watches the darkness that has haunted Eldermere for generations dissipate like smoke in a strong wind.

The stars emerge one by one, their light touching this cursed place for the first time in over a century.

The price of freedom has been paid. But as Marcus helps her to her feet, Clara knows the real work of healing is just beginning.

Some sacrifices break curses. Others break hearts. The hardest part is learning to live with both.

EPILOGUE

Months later, Eldermere has transformed.

The morning sun glints off the lighthouse's freshly painted walls. Its white tower and bright red rooftop stands proud against a clear blue sky.

Tour groups gather at its base, cameras flashing as guides share the town's remarkable history of redemption and renewal.

The fog still rolls in sometimes— natural now, carrying only the fresh scent of salt and sea.

Children play in its gentle swirls, their laughter replacing the whispers that once haunted these streets.

A new display prominently features Clara's book *Whispers in the Fog* in the window of the local bookshop.

The cover shows the majestic red roof and white pillars of the lighthouse emerging from the mist.

Inside, her words weave together the town's dark past and bright present, a testament to the power of truth and sacrifice.

The *New York Times bestseller* label glints on its jacket, but it's the letters from readers worldwide that mean the most to her—people finding hope in Eldermere's journey from darkness to light.

At the archives, now transformed into a historical center, Marcus helps visitors explore the town's intriguing history.

Sometimes, Clara joins him there, their hands finding each other as naturally as breathing.

Their relationship grows slowly and thoughtfully, built on the foundation of all they've faced together.

They still visit Oliver's memorial on quiet evenings, leaving flowers where the sea meets the shore.

His sacrifice taught Eldermere that the greatest acts of courage come not from hiding the truth, but from facing it head-on.

THE END